For my sweet daughter, Maddie.

And for Sarah Lyu, David DeWitt, and Jenna Pocius, for resonating with Quincy. Your collective passion for him brought him to life—thank you!

—BD

little bee books
an imprint of Bonnier Publishing USA

251 Park Avenue South, New York, NY 10010
Manufactured in China   HH 1217
First Edition   10 9 8 7 6 5 4 3 2 1
ISBN 978-1-4998-0542-0

Library of Congress Cataloging-in-Publication Data | Names: DiLorenzo, Barbara, author. | Title: Quincy / by Barbara DiLorenzo. | Description: First edition. | New York, NY: Little Bee Books, [2018] | Summary: Quincy wants to blend in at chameleon school but his daydreams always make him stand out, which is sometimes a good thing. | Identifiers: LCCN 2017004955 | Subjects: | CYAC: Individuality—Fiction. | Schools—Fiction. | Chameleons—Fiction. | Mural painting and decoration—Fiction. | Classification: LCC PZ7.1.D5635 Qui 2018 | DDC [E]—dc23 | LC record available at https://lccn.loc.gov/2017004955

littlebeebooks.com
bonnierpublishingusa.com

Quincy

THE CHAMELEON WHO COULDN'T BLEND IN

BARBARA DiLORENZO

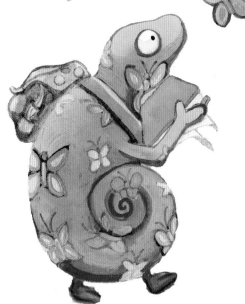

little bee books

Quincy wanted to love chameleon school.

He loved learning how to zap and eat flies with his sticky tongue.

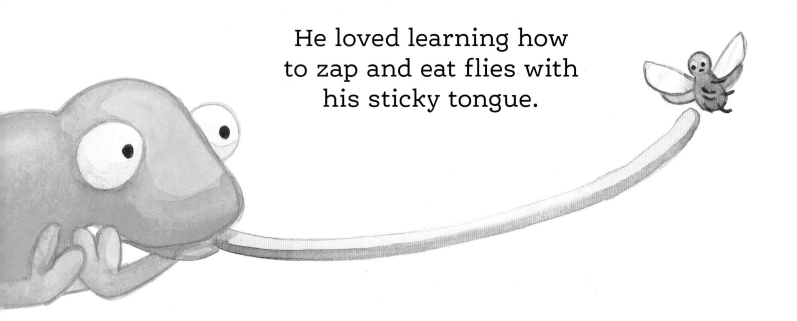

He was the best at rolling his eyes in all directions.

And nothing was better than swinging from his long, curly tail.

But there was one thing that Quincy wasn't good at . . .

Quincy's worst subject was camouflage.

"To be a leaf, you must *feel* like a leaf," said Miss Tanglewood.

Quincy just felt bored.
His mind wandered.

He noticed one leaf kind of
looked like a rocket ship.

Another looked
like a dinosaur.

And one looked
like a mustache.

"Quincy, please go to the Peace Corner
until you are ready to participate,"
said Miss Tanglewood.

Quincy's best subject was art because he loved painting. Mrs. Lin, his favorite teacher, showed the class how to paint leaves.

Suddenly,
he had an idea.

"I can paint myself
green and blend in with
the rest of the class!" he
said proudly.

The plan worked—at least until swim class.
He hoped that the paint was waterproof.

It wasn't.

"Quincy, go take a shower,"
grumbled Coach.

In the shower, Quincy closed his eyes and tried to clear his mind.

He tried to think of nothing.

But thinking of nothing reminded Quincy of clouds.

And clouds reminded him of rainbows.

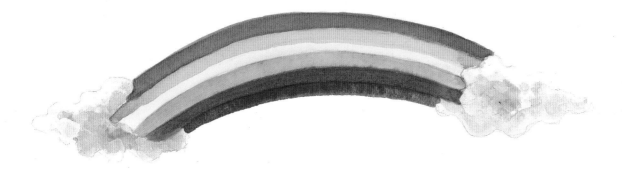

And rainbows reminded him of mountains.

At recess, Quincy was really bad at hide-and-seek.

He decided not to play anymore.

Instead, he sat alone, staring up at the clouds.
"Quincy, is everything okay?" Mrs. Lin asked.
"Yup," Quincy said.

"If you ever want to talk,
I'm here," she offered.

But after recess, Quincy realized he was not okay. He had completely forgotten that today was his turn to read his poem in front of the entire class!

He wished he could blend right into his seat.

But of course, he could not.

Quincy closed his eyes, took a deep breath, and tried to clear his mind.

He tried to focus on his poem, but he heard the audience whisper, and he felt their eyes on him. It occurred to Quincy that the worst thing he could think of right now . . .

. . . was that he had to pee.

Quincy ran offstage and into the art room.

Mrs. Lin asked, "Are you sure you're okay, Quincy?"

"No matter what I do, I can't blend in,"
said Quincy.

"Hmmm," said Mrs. Lin.

"You may have trouble blending in," said Mrs. Lin, "but that's okay. Look at what you can do!"

Quincy couldn't help but smile.

"We have a playground wall that needs painting," Mrs. Lin said. "Would you like to paint your very own mural?"

Quincy beamed. "Yes!"

The next day, Quincy gathered all his art supplies.

He closed his eyes. Instead of clearing his mind, he let his imagination wander.

And he thought about how the world can be a beautiful place.

Quincy knew what to paint.

He painted what was on his mind.

His classmates were curious
what he was up to. They watched
him work every day. He was so busy,
he hadn't noticed the crowd
gathered behind him.

"Wow," they said.

Quincy was as colorful as ever.

But for once . . .

. . . he didn't mind.

Author's Note

Though Quincy is a fictional character, his color changing isn't unlike what real chameleons do. A popular misconception is that these lizards change their skin color to resemble their background, to blend in and avoid predators. But chameleons have other ways to stay safe. For example, they can walk with a shaky stride that, from afar, resembles a leaf blowing in the breeze. They can also use their long tongues to nab tasty bugs for meals, which minimizes their movement so they are less obvious to predators.

Scientists now believe that chameleons sometimes change colors to reflect how they feel. For example, when they are calm, chameleons are green, but when angry, some species of chameleon flash bright yellow. When they are in love, some chameleons turn bright turquoise and display various patterns on their skin.

Animals that do attempt to match their skin to their surroundings for the purpose of camouflage are flatfish like flounder, as well as cephalopods—octopus, squid, and cuttlefish.

While our ability is mostly limited to turning red in the face when embarrassed, we humans can also alter our skin color to match our emotions!